# Den 4
## Meets
## the Jinx

# Den 4 Meets the Jinx

## Kathy Kennedy Tapp

Margaret K. McElderry Books

NEW YORK

*Special thanks to Aaron C.*

Copyright © 1988 by Kathy Kennedy Tapp

All rights reserved. No part of this book may be reproduced or transmitted in any form or by any means, electronic or mechanical, including photocopying, recording, or by any information storage and retrieval system, without permission in writing from the Publisher.

Margaret K. McElderry Books
Macmillan Publishing Company
866 Third Avenue, New York, NY 10022
Collier Macmillan Canada, Inc.

Composition by Haddon Craftsmen
Allentown, Pennsylvania
Printed and bound by R. R. Donnelley & Sons
Harrisonburg, Virginia
Designed by Cathryn S. Aison
First Edition
10  9  8  7  6  5  4  3  2  1

Library of Congress Cataloging-in-Publication Data
Tapp, Kathy Kennedy.
Den 4 meets the jinx/Kathy Kennedy Tapp.—1st ed.
p.  cm.
Summary: Despairing over the fact that his bratty five-year-old sister, Jessie, ruins everything he tries to do with his Cub Scout den, Adam never suspects that she may be the only person who can save the den from dissolving.
ISBN 0-689-50453-5
[1. Cub Scouts—Fiction. 2. Brothers and sisters—Fiction.]
I. Title. II. Title: Den four meets the jinx.
PZ7.T1646De  1988    [Fic]—dc19  88–12776  CIP  AC

*To Katrina, who once searched for golden eggs,
and also to Bonnie Joy*

# Contents

# Den 4
# Meets
# the Jinx

# 1
# October: The Cub Scout Magic Show

"No!" Adam yelled. "No, no, no—for the tenth time, *no!* It's our magic show and you can't be in it!"

"I can too!" Jessie waved the orange knee sock tied around her neck. "See my scarf? I'm a Scub Scout, too!"

"*Cub* Scout!" Adam stamped his foot. "And your dumb old sock doesn't look *anything* like a real Cub Scout scarf!" He took off his black magician cape and set it on one of the chairs lining the walls of the living room.

"Scub Scout, Scub Scout," sang Jessie, jump-

I

ing up and down. The top part of her hair stuck out like porcupine prickles from the haircut she'd given herself two days before. Then she stopped jumping and stared at Adam's cape.

Uh-oh. Adam knew that stare. A danger signal. When Jessie stared hard at something like that, it meant that her two brain cells were going round and round in her head. Plotting. Scheming.

He put his hand on his cape, protectively. "*Our* magic show," he said again, glaring his fiercest glare. "Understand?" He reached into his pocket and pulled out a tiny yellow plastic box. It was supposed to be a refrigerator for a dollhouse, but Adam kept tiny rolled-up spit wads in it. He'd traded it from Steven for three comic books. He opened the little plastic door and pulled out a spit wad and his straw shooter.

"Mom!" Jessie squealed. "Adam's gonna shoot a spit wad at me!"

"That's enough, you two!" Mom hurried in from the kitchen. "Jessie, you can *watch* the show. Adam, is everything all set for your trick? The other Scouts will be here any minute."

"It's all ready." Adam waved his arm toward his cape proudly. "All except for a light. We need a little light; not the regular lamp."

"How about a night-light?" Mom said. "Either yours or Jessie's."

"Adam has a night-light!" teased a voice at the front door. Trevor Jones. Big fat Trevor, with curly hair and freckles. "Adam has a night-light!"

Adam's face turned red. He lunged for the door.

"Oh yeah?" he yelled. "Wanna make something of it?"

Trevor's face disappeared from the screen. Adam raced down the trailer steps after him.

"Adam! Come back here! There'll be no fighting!" Mom ran out of the trailer. Jessie started to follow, then she stopped. She stared at the cape again, then at the card table in the middle of the room. It was all set up for the magic show, with a blanket covering it and a magic wand sitting on top.

"I can too do tricks," Jessie said softly. "I can do tricks as good as Adam."

She picked up the cape. It was black and shiny and it had a secret pocket inside, with a toy rabbit hidden in the pocket. Carefully she pulled out the little stuffed bunny.

"And now ladies and gentlemen," Jessie whispered, throwing the cape around her shoulders, "I will do the most *amazingest* trick. I will pull a bunny out of . . ."

"Come on, everyone! Time to start the magic show!" Adam yelled. He was right outside the trailer door. Jessie yanked off the cape and threw it on the chair.

"I'm going first! My trick first!" yelled Kyle.

The front door opened. Jessie looked around frantically. Then, as the Scouts started pouring in the front door, she dived beneath the blanket and under the card table.

"Boys! Boys! Find a seat! It's time to begin the magic show!" Mom clapped her hands.

"Wait'll you see my trick!" Michael bragged.

"It won't be as good as mine." Adam grinned, then grabbed Kyle by his jacket pocket and pulled him down on the floor, tumbling.

"Adam, get up off that floor." Mom's voice already sounded tired. "I've told you before—our living room is *not* a wrestling mat! Find a seat."

"My trick's the best!" Trevor called out.

"Disappear, Trevor. That'd be the best trick."

Adam gave a quick glance around the room. Good. Jessie was nowhere in sight.

"I'll go first," Kyle ran over to the card table. He cleared his throat and stood there, grinning at everyone. "Oops, wait a minute. I forgot my magic duck." He raced over to one of the chairs and grabbed up a piece of yellow cardboard.

"See this duck?" He held it out. "It's *magic*."

"You call that cardboard thing a *duck*?"

"Yeah, and it's going to lay a magic golden egg," Kyle announced proudly. "Now, I'll just say the magic word, abracadabra . . . and, uh . . ." His voice drew out the word while he pulled at the back of the cardboard. "Uh . . . I'll just say the magic word again. . . ."

Adam started giggling. Kyle looked so funny, all red-faced, his hands obviously trying to pull something out from behind the stupid cardboard.

"Hey, Kyle, where's the magic egg?" Steven yelled.

"Uh . . . uh . . ." Kyle was giggling now, too. "I guess it's so magic, it already disappeared!"

"Sure, sure. Sit down, Kyle!" Trevor yelled.

"It's here somewhere!" Kyle yelled back. "Somebody will find the golden egg and get all the magic!"

"My turn!" Adam jumped up. "*Now* you'll see some magic!" He drew on his cape, swirling it around him. He held up the black hat.

"And now, ladies and gentlemen," he declared, "you see this hat. . . ." He turned it upside down to show that it was empty. "When I say the magic word, a rabbit will come out of this very hat."

"I bet it has a fake bottom!" yelled Steven.

"Yeah. Let us feel the hat," Trevor called.

Adam shrugged and tossed him the hat. "Suit yourself," he said smugly. The rabbit wasn't hidden in the hat; it was in a secret pocket of his trusty magician's cape.

Trevor punched his fist down the hat.

"Hey, I said you could *feel* it, not break it!" Adam yanked the hat away, glaring. Stupid Trevor. "And now," he continued solemnly, "I'll say the magic word, and before your very eyes a rabbit shall appear!" His voice babbled on, while his other hand felt around inside his cape for the secret pocket. "Abracadabra . . ." The pocket felt flat. There wasn't a bulge where the toy rabbit was supposed to be. A funny feeling pulled at his stomach; a feeling like staring at a test paper and not knowing any of the answers. Panic rushed to his face in a hot flood. "Uh . . . uh . . ." he stammered.

And then he felt a tug on his leg.

"Adam," came a loud whisper from under the table. "It's down here. The bunny's down here." Another tug on his leg.

6

"It's here, Adam." The whisper was even louder now. Every single person in the room could hear it. "Here's the bunny." A little arm reached up, pushing the rabbit up on the card table.

Giggles broke out all around the room.

"Here's the bunny, Adam!"

"Who's your assistant, Adam?"

"Adam, you got somebody hiding under the table?"

"*Great* trick, Adam!"

For a second, Adam stood there, feeling kind of dazed. Then another feeling rushed through him. He reached down and yanked up the edge of the tablecloth.

"Hi," Jessie whispered. Then, "Uh-oh." She scrambled out from under the table, bringing the tablecloth with her, just as Adam lunged.

Jessie shot toward the door. Adam vaulted over the card table after her. "You little—"

And then the whole den was on its feet.

"Come on, after her!"

"Last one out's a rotten egg!"

"When I get her, she's gonna be dead. I mean *dead.*"

"Boys!" Mom yelled. "Come back here!" But Adam kept running, past the Abernathys' trailer, around Miss Lynn's trailer, behind the manager's trailer. He kept his eyes peeled for signs of crooked spiky hair, an orange neck, and brown overalls.

"Did anyone see which way she went?"

"Over there—" Kyle pointed.

"I thought she went *that* way," Josh cried.

"OK, let's try that." Adam took the trash cans in a flying leap. His heart was thumping in his ears; his legs felt ready to do the Boston Marathon. The angry feeling had somehow become a crazy excitement, as he dodged bushes and bikes and raced between trailers.

"The field! Try the field!"

They charged through the trailer court playground toward the weed field.

"ADAM! KYLE! STEVEN! JOSHUA! TREVOR! MICHAEL! Stop this instant!" Mom ran up to Adam. Her hand clamped on his arm.

"Adam Simpson, you head back to the trailer *this instant!*" She shook his arm. "Do you understand me? And bring the rest of them with you. I'm thoroughly ashamed of you!"

Adam stopped obediently. But his eyes kept searching, through the weeds of the field. She was probably hiding out there somewhere, in the weeds or dried up cornstalks.

"Do you understand me?" Mom repeated, shaking his arm.

"Yes," Adam said. Then, under his breath, "But when she gets back, she's gonna be *dead.*"

# 2
# The Headhunter

"She ruined my trick! She ruined the whole magic show! She's ruining my whole life!"

He said it to Mom. He said it to Dad when he got home from work. He said it at dinner, to his mashed potatoes and his pork chops, and then to his cereal the next morning. All his birthday money had gone to buy that cape with the special hidden pocket and the rabbit. It would have been the best trick of all. *Would* have been. Except for Jessie the Jinx.

"She ruined the whole meeting. She ruined—"

"All *right!*" Mom said finally. "Adam, drop it. Jessie's been punished for what she did."

"No dessert after dinner," Jessie chanted, sliding into the kitchen on her holey pj feet, with her stupid orange knee sock still tied around her neck. "And I had to stay in my room *all* last night." She climbed in her seat. "I was only just trying to *help* your trick."

"You're about as much help as the measles."

"She should be in school," Dad said in a low voice to Mom. "Then she wouldn't be always tagging along after Adam."

"I want to go to school." Jessie set down her spoon. "I'm five. Five-year-olds go to school! I want to go."

"Your birthday's too late, honey," Mom said. "You'll get to go to kindergarten next year."

"With all the kids in this trailer court, how come there aren't any other five-year-olds?" asked Dad.

"I want to go to school." Once Jessie got started on something, she never shut up. "I *need* to go to school."

"You *need* to go to jail," Adam cut in. "You need to be in a big cage and the key should be flushed down the toilet! You're a jinx. Jinxes belong in jail."

"I am not a jinx. . . ." Jessie stopped. "What's a jinx?"

"A pest. A troublemaker. A person who brings bad luck—"

"The problem isn't just Jessie," Mom said. She turned to Dad. "This trailer is just too small for Scout meetings. You should have *seen* those kids yesterday; like a herd of wild buffalo all over the trailer court. The manager told me he got several complaints. I've decided to tell the scoutmaster to look for another den leader. Someone with a basement."

"Sure." Dad grinned. "Now where have I heard that before?"

"I mean it this time," Mom said firmly. "Enough's enough. Having a meeting of nine and ten-year-old boys in this trailer is like holding a rodeo in a playpen. They'll have to find another place."

"Good," said Adam. "Then we can have our meetings without *her* around." He grabbed his lunch box off the counter. "Bye. Have to catch the bus."

"I'm going to school, too." Jessie scrambled up after him. "I'm going to catch the bus, too!"

Adam groaned and shot out the door and over to the row of mailboxes where all the trailer court kids waited for the school bus. Kyle was already there.

"Hey, Adam, the Haunted House opens tonight at the old warehouse. Only costs fifty cents. Want to go?"

"Nah." Adam tried to sound casual. Like he didn't care one way or the other. "They're dumb. Stupid fake monsters. Waste of money."

"What do you mean? It was *great* last year!" Kyle tossed his lunch box in the air. "Remember the vampire that tried to grab you when you went around the corner? And the headless ghost in the bathtub?"

"Nah," Adam said again, kicking at the mailbox post. "It's stupid. And . . . I have to go someplace tonight, anyway," he lied. He sure *did* remember the vampire and all the bloodcurdling screams in the dark hallways. No way was he paying to go back in that creepy dark warehouse. "Stupid," he growled again and spat into the weeds.

Steven came running over from his trailer. "Hey, wasn't that a great chase yesterday?" he called out. "Chasing your sister was the best thing we've done in Scouts so far!"

"Yeah," Kyle nodded. "I jumped over two trash cans and didn't even wipe out!"

"Jessie sure wrecked your trick," Steven said cheerfully.

"Yeah," Adam scowled. Speaking of the Jinx, there she was, skipping down the walkway with her orange knee sock around her neck. She was pushing a toy wheelbarrow with her doll in it.

"I'm going to school too," Jessie called out. "Me and Waffle Ann. This is our school bus."

Steven stared at the doll in the cart. "Wow, what happened to her face?"

Jessie sighed. "I always have to tell *everyone* about it. She used to be Raggedy Ann. But I was playing restaurant and I was pretending the waffle iron was the hamburger bun and Raggedy Ann's head was the hamburger."

"And the waffle iron was still hot," Adam cut in. "So she's been Waffle Ann ever since."

"Yep," Jessie agreed, holding up the doll proudly.

"Wow." Steven said again. He reached down to touch the scorch marks. "You're lucky the cloth didn't catch fire."

"Wrecks her dolls just like she wrecks magic shows," Adam muttered. "She beheaded her other doll a few weeks ago."

Kyle poked him. "Speaking of magic shows, did you find your 'magic' rabbit?"

"Did you find your 'magic' duck egg?" Adam shot back, grinning.

"I *told* you," Kyle said. "It was such a magic golden egg, it disappeared again. Maybe it's hiding in the field."

Jessie pushed her wheelbarrow up closer to Kyle. "Is there a real magic golden egg in the field, Kyle?" Jessie said in a hushed voice. She stared out into the field. *The* stare. Danger sign. "How big is it?" she whispered.

"It's really big and golden and . . . and the person who finds it gets all the magic," Kyle said, holding his hand up close to his mouth to hide the grin.

"Me and Waffle Ann are going to find it," said Jessie. She turned and spat into the weeds. "My spit goes almost as far as yours does," she bragged. "I can spit and I can find golden duck eggs." She grabbed the wheelbarrow handles and turned toward the field.

"You better be careful," Adam said. "There's probably *danger* out there." He made his voice low and mysterious. "Look—there's something now." He pointed at a tall figure moving through the weeds.

"That's just Mr. Saunders," Kyle said. "He's back from his hunting trip and . . . hey, look,

Adam—he's got a deer head!" He started waving his arms. "Hey, Mr. Saunders, can we see your deer head?"

The tall figure in the orange vest strode toward them. "Six point buck," Mr. Saunders called out proudly, holding up the deer head. "Just got it back from the taxidermist."

"Wow." Adam stared, fascinated, at the great head, the glassy eyes, the huge antlers.

He heard a little shriek behind him.

Jessie's eyes were enormous and round. In a panicky, high-pitched voice, she whispered, "Branches. It's . . . got branches. . . ."

"It's a head," Adam said wickedly. "A *dead* head. . . ."

"Mr. Saunders is a headhunter," Kyle said.

Jessie's eyes got even rounder. She looked from the deer head to Mr. Saunders. Grabbing Waffle Ann out of the wheelbarrow, she took off madly toward the trailer, screaming all the way.

# 3
# The Butter Monster
# and the Teddy Bear Trailer

"Jessie, there aren't any heads in your room," Mom said for the fifth time. "And it's time for you to go to bed."

"I'm going to dream about heads. I already dreamed about them three times! I don't want to go to bed!" Jessie whimpered.

Adam looked up from the rope he was trying to tie in a square knot. "It was just a dumb deer head," he said scornfully. "All week she's been fussing about it!"

"It had branches growing out of it!" Jessie cried.

"The man you saw the other day was Bruce Saunders," Mom said patiently. "He hunts. I don't think deer heads are very nice decorations either. But they can't hurt you." She scooped Jessie up. "Now. Time for bed. I'll sit with you for a little while, OK?"

"Just a dumb deer head," Adam muttered again. He gave one last tug on the rope. There. A perfect square knot. He flipped on the TV and plopped down on the floor cushion with a sigh. This was his favorite time of night. The Jinx was in bed, his homework was done, and his favorite show was on.

It was during the third or fourth commercial that he heard the yell.

"It's after me! It's after me!"

Jessie came flying down the hall and into the living room. "It's gonna get me!"

Dad and Mom ran in. Adam jumped up. "Jessie . . ." Mom began, but Jessie ran past them all as if they weren't even there, and charged into the kitchen. "It's gonna get me!" she shrieked, bumping into a chair.

"Sleepwalking," Dad said, hurrying after her. "She's having a nightmare."

"She's . . . *asleep*!" Adam cried incredulously.

How could someone who was yelling and running around with wide-open eyes be asleep?

"There it is!" Jessie yelled, running over to the kitchen table. "I'll get it!" She banged her fist down on the cube of butter sitting in its butter dish. "Gotcha!" she cried, whamming her fist into the soft golden cube, turning it into a mushy mess. SPLAT, THUMP, SPLOSH, SQUISH.

"Jessie—" Mom's voice was low, gentle. "Let's go back to bed, honey."

Jessie just kept pounding. Adam watched in amazement. Nobody—not even Jessie—tried to attack a stick of butter! The Jinx had flipped for good!

"Yuk!" Jessie's voice changed; she stared at her fingers, all greasy yellow, smeared with soft butter. "It's dead!" she sobbed. She tried to shake her fingers clean. "I killed it!"

Adam felt a giant giggle working its way up.

"Jessie, honey, come with me." Mom took her by the shoulders, guiding her to the sink to wash her hands.

"I killed it!" Jessie whimpered again, staring at her fingers.

"Yes, yes," Mom said soothingly. "Now let's go to bed. . . ."

"She killed the butter." The giggle was out. "Jessie killed the butter!" The giggles got bigger, louder, rolling through Adam so hard that he fell back against the counter. He let his legs slide out from under him. He plopped onto the floor, grabbing his stomach. "Ooof," he gasped. "Jessie killed the butter!"

"Congratulations," Adam said to Jessie at breakfast. He gave her a big grin.

"What?" Jessie looked up in surprise.

"Congratulations on killing the butter." Adam started to giggle and then choked on his toast.

Jessie stared at him. Then she pointed her finger at Adam, then at her ear, drawing little circles in the air. "Cuckoo," she said.

"She doesn't even know she did it!" Adam cried in disbelief.

"You had a nightmare," Mom told Jessie. "You walked in your sleep."

"She did more than walk!"

"I didn't either," Jessie cried. "When I sleep, I lay in my bed. I can't walk with my eyes closed."

"They were open," Adam assured her. "And you tried to kill the butter." Still giggling, he jumped up and grabbed his lunch box.

"I didn't either try to kill the butter!" Jessie yelled after him.

"Lots of people walk in their sleep now and then," Mom said. "It was just a bad dream, Jessie. Don't worry about it." She reached over and patted Jessie's spiky head. "What you need to do, young lady, is to think about something else. Something *nice*—like visiting Miss Lynn this afternoon."

"Miss Lynn! I get to visit the teddy bear trailer!" Jessie jumped up from her seat.

Adam turned his head away, so Jessie couldn't see his smirk. It was all part of the plan. Today was Wednesday—Cub Scout day. And *this time* Jessie was going to be safely at Miss Lynn's during the whole meeting. So she wouldn't even be home and she couldn't wreck the meeting. She could play with the zillion teddy bears Miss Lynn kept all over her trailer, instead. His grin got bigger. He headed out the door, whistling. "Bye everyone!"

At school, Steven called out, "Hey, Adam, do we get to chase your sister again at the meeting? That was great last time!"

"Nope!" Adam tossed his notebook in the air cheerfully. "The Jinx is going to disappear this time. And we're going to work on the talent show. I'm doing a monster movie. Mark Wood-man is going to help me."

The day had started out great, and it just kept getting better. At recess he got a home run, at lunch he traded his peanut butter sandwich for a piece of cold pizza, and he got a package of Twinkies free, because Kyle didn't want them and his candy bar, too. Then there were donut holes at the Scout meeting. Mark came over after that to start the plans for the monster movie.

The world was a lovely place without the Jinx. Adam whistled all the way down to Miss Lynn's trailer to pick up Jessie.

He could hear Miss Lynn's voice as he started up the walkway.

"This is a dumb book, Jessie." Miss Lynn sounded disgusted. "As if that princess didn't have anything to do but figure out if there was a stupid pea under her bed. Princesses should *do* things. Go on quests, seek their fortunes, kill dragons!"

Adam stepped around the teddy bear tied in a wagon on the porch and banged the teddy bear knocker.

"Come on in, Adam." Miss Lynn came to the door, her pretty long hair fluffing around her face.

"Jessie and I have been playing school. I'm the teacher."

Adam stepped into a room full of teddy bears. There were two on the sofa with Jessie, some on bookshelves, some on the counter in the kitchen, along with a cassette player, and three or four on Miss Lynn's big desk that took up half her living room. Besides teddy bears, it was also heaped with college books.

"We've been reading my old fairy tale book," Miss Lynn said. "And I'm finding I don't like it nearly as much as I did as a little girl." She laughed. "The princesses are a bunch of wimps."

Jessie sat plopped on the sofa, staring at the book.

"Go away, Adam. I'm reading," she said sternly. "I'm very busy. I'm reading all the words. This is a very big person story." She turned the page and then she squealed and started bouncing on the couch. "Miss Lynn, Miss Lynn, it's the golden duck egg! It's right here! I found it—a big gold egg, just like Kyle said!"

From the way she was yelling you'd have thought a solid gold egg was stuck to the page. Adam peered over her shoulder.

It was just an old-fashioned fancy picture of

23

an egg, with some fairy tale people gawking at it. No big deal.

"Now I know what it *really* looks like!" Jessie was still bouncing excitedly. "I can find it now. Kyle says it's probably in the field and I'm going to find it!"

"Why not?" Miss Lynn laughed again. "That'd be a great quest for a princess. Finding a golden egg is much more adventurous than finding a pea under a mattress!"

"I'm going to—" Jessie stopped. She stared at Adam. She dropped the book and stood up on the couch.

"Is it Wednesday?" she cried, with a little quiver in her voice. She grabbed Adam's arm. "Is it?"

Rats. He'd forgotten to change out of his uniform!

"Uh . . ." he stammered. He couldn't think of a lie quick enough. But a lie wouldn't work anyway. She knew.

"I missed the Scub Scout meeting!" Jessie howled and raced out the front door for home.

# 4
# November: The Cub Scout Talent Show

"It was not a trick," Mom said firmly. "You had a nice afternoon with Miss Lynn, and the Cub Scouts had their meeting, too."

"It was too a trick," Adam said gleefully. "And it worked. We had a great meeting, Jessie." He picked up an orange from the fruit bowl and tossed it in the air. "Mom, guess what? Mark's going to help me make a monster movie for the talent show!" Mark knew all about making movies. He was twelve and he had his own Super-8 movie camera. They'd make a *great* movie! Adam turned toward Jessie, hunching his shoulders, spreading out his arms. "Ooligans," he hissed. "It's gonna be a movie about ooligans. Big ug-lee ooooligaan-monsters with *fangs* . . ."

Jessie screamed and grabbed Mom's leg.

"That's enough, Adam!"

Adam grinned and stomped down the hall. He turned around in his doorway. "Too bad you missed the meeting, Jessie. We had a great treat. Kyle brought donut holes."

"I want a donut hole!" Jessie wailed. "I want to be in the movie!"

Adam ignored her and turned into his room, whistling. Things were looking great. The movie would be terrific. And they were going to start shooting it tomorrow, first thing after school!

"Put more fake blood on your face, Adam," Mark yelled, working the focus on the camera. "It'll look really bloody then, when I use the zoom lens for a close-up."

Adam squeezed the tube of fake blood. Red gooey stuff oozed onto his finger. "Good thing I've got so much left from Halloween," he said, smearing it over his cheeks. "Now for the fangs." Those were left over from Halloween, too. They even glowed in the dark.

"You need a black cape," Mark said, studying him. "A Dracula ooligan!"

"I can use my magician's cape! It's black." Adam raced back to the trailer to get it.

Adam let the cape swirl across his shoulders. He felt terrifically wicked. The movie would be so good that they'd probably even get to show it at the Blue and Gold Banquet in February! He took a flying leap down the trailer steps.

"Let's go out in the field and shoot the first scene," Mark yelled.

Adam started to run after him; then he stopped and cast one last look around. *She'd* better not be anywhere in sight, if she knew what was good for her. This was one thing she was *not* going to butt in on.

"Swoop!" yelled Mark, aiming his camera. "Swoop and make faces. Swirl your cape. Great!"

Adam dived and swirled and made ugly big-fanged grins and howled at the sky. Mark's camera whirred and clicked.

"It's fantastic!" he called. "Hey, I've got an idea for a *great* scene. Get up in that tree over there. See that branch that goes way out? You can stand on the branch and jump down. I'll shoot you in midair!"

Adam looked at the tree. It was one of those that grew wild in the field. None of the branches were very thick. The one Mark had pointed to was high. And super thin. His stomach did a little flip.

"You'll look like you're flying, Adam!"

Adam took a few steps toward the tree. He turned back toward Mark. "If I climb up there I'll tear the cape," he said in a low voice.

"Not if you're careful."

Adam walked closer to the tree. He stared up at the branch. Close up, it looked even higher.

"No," he said. His voice was low, stubborn.

"Hey, what's the big deal?" Mark asked. "It's just a little old tree."

"*No.*" Adam glared at Mark. He clenched his fists by his sides. "It'd be a dumb scene. It wouldn't look like I was flying. It'd look like I was falling."

"OK, OK. Forget it." Mark sounded disgusted. Adam looked back up at the tree. He wanted to climb it; he really wanted to . . . but his stomach knotted into a square knot at the thought of going up high places, or into dark places. He hated his stomach for being such a sissy; hated the shaky scared feeling. Wasn't there someplace else they could shoot a flying scene? He looked around desperately, then he noticed something moving in the weeds. Something with curly brown hair and an orange sock around its neck.

"JESSIE!" he yelled. "I see you!"

The brown hair and the orange sock popped up. "I wanna be in the movie too!"

Adam turned away from the tree. The sissy feeling fled and the ooligan feeling came back. He moved toward Jessie, swooping, flapping his arms, growling. "You ... can't be ... in the movie ... and if you don't ... get out ... of here right now ... the ooooligaaans *will eat you up!*"

Her eyes got huge. A squeal popped out of her mouth. She took off like a streak toward home.

Adam felt much better. Not that he was ever *glad* to see the Jinx—but now he felt properly ferocious again. He grinned triumphantly at Mark. Who cared about an old tree limb, anyway?

# 5
# *The Ooligans*

"Now, Adam, Dad and I will only be gone for an hour or so," Mom said, putting on her coat. "Remember, Mark's in charge. Jessie's asleep and you boys can watch TV or work on your movie inside. Here's the phone number where we'll be."

"Good-bye," Adam mumbled, never taking his eyes off the TV set.

In her bedroom, Jessie sat up, wide awake.

"We have ooligan baby-sitters," she whispered, grabbing Waffle Ann. She turned on the light over her bed.

"Last time we dreamed about headhunters.

This time we might dream about ooligans. We might try to kill the butter again!"

This would be a terrible time to dream about ooligans. Mark and Adam wouldn't say, "That's all right, Jessie. There isn't any such thing as ooligans." Mark and Adam *liked* ooligans. Adam *was* an ooligan.

There was only one thing to do.

"Waffle Ann, we won't go to sleep tonight," Jessie whispered, sitting Waffle Ann up straight against the pillow. "We won't even shut our eyes."

That was not a problem for Waffle Ann. But after a little while Jessie's eyes started to feel— silly. She yawned.

"We'll listen to TV," she whispered. "It's real loud. It'll keep us awake."

In the living room, Mark got up off the floor and stretched when the detective show switched to a commercial. "Hey, Adam, am I supposed to check on Jessie? I never watched anyone her age before."

"Don't let her know that," Adam advised him. "But you don't have to worry tonight. When she falls asleep, even the smoke alarm can't wake her up. The batteries went wacko one night and everyone else was running around covering their

31

ears and the Jinx didn't even hear it."

"Okay then," Mark settled back down. "Got anything good to eat?"

"I'll go look." Adam headed for the kitchen, then stopped and stared.

Jessie was sitting on the kitchen floor with a bag of peanuts opened and spread out all around her. She was banging the salt shaker down on a peanut to crack its shell. There were pieces of peanut shells all over the floor.

"What are you doing?" Adam yelled. "You're supposed to be in bed asleep!"

Mark ran in. "I thought you said she'd sleep through anything!"

"I didn't go to sleep," Jessie mumbled through a mouthful of peanuts. "Me and Waffle Ann are going to stay awake all night."

"No you're not!" Adam said. "Or I'll tell Mom and Dad when they get home."

"We don't want to dream about ooligans," Jessie opened her mouth in a wide yawn; some peanut pieces fell out. "I'm staying awake—like Daddy does." She banged another shell open. "With peanuts."

"Huh?" said Mark. "What does that mean?"

Adam sighed. "When we go on vacation, when Dad's driving at night, he brings peanuts to chew. He says it keeps him awake. So . . ." He waved his arm toward Jessie and the mess on the floor, then shook his head. "But *he* brings the kind that are shelled."

Mark turned to Jessie. "Look. You have to go to bed." Adam could tell from the way he said it that Mark wasn't used to baby-sitting. He didn't know how to order little kids around.

"Here," Adam told him, "you do it like *this*." He knelt down by Jessie and made his voice low and threatening. "If you don't go to bed right now, you won't get any dessert the whole rest of the week. Mom said."

"You're not the boss of me!" Jessie said, but she got up, grabbing her doll. She walked two steps toward her room, then turned and looked back.

"Go!" ordered Adam.

Jessie took two more steps, then turned around again. She gave Mark a little sly smile.

"*Go!*" Adam stomped his foot. Then, as Jessie disappeared into her room, he turned to Mark. "*That's* how you handle little kids. Got to let them know who's boss."

"I guess . . . we should clean up the floor, huh?" Mark stared at the peanut mess.

"Nah. The show's back on. We can do it

later." Adam grabbed the rest of the peanuts and plopped down on the living room rug.

A few minutes later they heard a big thud and a scream.

"I dropped him!" Jessie yelled. "I dropped Pinocchio!"

"The goldfish—" Adam raced toward her room. What the heck was she doing with Pinocchio? The fishbowl was supposed to be on the hall shelf.

It wasn't on the hall shelf. It was upside down on Jessie's rug. There was water all over the place. And the Jinx was sitting in a big soggy puddle yelling, "I dropped him! I dropped him!"

"Jessie!" Adam cried, *"What are you doing?"*

"I just didn't want to dream about ooligans!" Jessie sobbed.

"Adam, get some towels, quick!" Mark yelled. He bent over, cupping his hands around slippery Pinocchio, who was flopping on the rug. "There! Gotcha!"

"Don't squish him!" Jessie cried. "Don't strangle him!"

"Dumb," Adam muttered, stomping towels over the wet spots on the rug. He glared at Jessie, scrunched down on her bed in her soggy nightgown. "What'd you try to carry the fishbowl for?"

34

"I just didn't want to dream about ooligans!"

Mark grabbed the fishbowl and ran into the bathroom.

"What the heck does a goldfish have to do with *ooligans*?" he shouted over the running water.

"Pinocchio never shuts his eyes," Jessie said. "So me and Waffle Ann were going to watch him and learn how to keep our eyes open." Tears ran down her face. "We didn't want to dream about ooligans." She started crying louder. "They're ugly and scary and it's all your fault! You should've made nicer ooligans! Then me and Waffle Ann could shut our eyes!"

"Oh sure. Nice ooligans," Adam snorted. "That'd make a great movie."

"Forget about ooligans, would you!" Mark cried. "Go back to bed." He looked out the window. "Your mom and dad'll be mad if they find out about this."

Adam shook his head. Mark was a great movie director, but he was a lousy baby-sitter. *Never* let a little kid know you're nervous and that you don't know what to do.

Sure enough, Jessie stopped crying and stared at Mark, hard. *The* stare. The two brain cells were twirling around. . . .

"Well . . ." she said finally in a sad little voice, "I might be able to shut my eyes and go to sleep if there could be a pretty ooligan in your movie. An ooligan princess. I'd probably dream about her. I'd probably go to sleep right now. If the ooligan princess could wear her Easter dress. And a crown."

"NO!" Adam shouted. "No, no, double *no!* You're not butting in on our movie!!"

There was the sound of a car pulling into the driveway. Mark looked toward the window, then over at Jessie.

"I'll go right to sleep," Jessie said with a little sniffle. "And I won't tell Mommy and Daddy about Pinocchio . . . if I can be in your movie. . . ."

"All right!" Mark growled. "*One* scene. Just *one* scene, you hear? *Now go to sleep!*"

"No!" Adam hollered. Mark grabbed his arm and pulled him out of the room.

"Don't worry. It's no big deal. We'll just give her two and a half seconds. Okay?"

"First she ruined the magic show, and now she's gonna ruin the movie!" Adam yelled all the way down the hall. But Jessie didn't hear. She lay back obediently in bed, even though her pajamas were damp and bumpy with peanut shells.

"Waffle Ann," she whispered into the darkness, "we're gonna be in their movie after all. We're gonna be ooligan princesses!"

# 6
# The Princess Scene

"It won't be so bad, Adam," Mark said for the twentieth time.

"Sure," Adam growled. Old Jessie the Jinx had done it again; butted into his life, his projects, his fun.

"Look, Adam," Mark set down his camera, "with Jessie in it you can have a real *victim*. You can really chase someone. It'll make the movie more exciting."

"Sure," Adam muttered. But he thought about Mark's words. He looked at Jessie, just coming out of the trailer in a silly lacy dress, with a yellow paper crown flopping over her eyebrows. She was dragging her doll with the tic-tac-toe face.

Maybe Mark was right. So far they'd just been shooting Adam in his cape and fangs, swooping around. They'd made some clay monsters and used the zoom lens to try and make them look life sized. But Jessie really was life sized. And she knew how to scream and holler when she was scared. He chewed his bubble gum thoughtfully. Maybe this wouldn't be such a bad scene after all. He could chase her, wave his cape at her, swoop down. . . .

Actually this might be the most fun scene of the whole movie!

"Come over here," Mark yelled to Jessie. "Put your doll down."

"But Waffle Ann wants to be in the movie, too!" Jessie ran over, dragging her doll.

"Your doll's not going to be in the movie and neither are you, if you don't shut up!" Adam yelled.

"All *right*," Jessie stomped her foot. "You don't have to yell. My ears aren't broke, you know." She pushed her crown down on her head. Then she walked over closer to Mark. "What's on your teeth?"

"Braces," Mark said, adjusting the camera. "Just got 'em on."

Jessie just stood there, staring. "Do they hurt?" she asked, leaning over so close she was practically standing on his shoes.

"Quit staring," Mark scowled. "Haven't you ever seen braces before? Get ready for the scene."

"Hey, guys," Kyle came running over from his trailer. "Can I watch you shoot your movie?"

"I'm going to be in the movie too, Kyle!" Jessie shouted.

"The Jinx strikes again." Adam tried to sound like he was still mad, but it didn't work. "And in this next scene, ladies and gentlemen, the ooligan *zaps* the Jinx!" he ended cheerfully.

"Kyle, I didn't find the golden duck egg yet," Jessie called.

"Huh?" asked Kyle blankly.

Adam nudged him. "The egg—remember? Your magic trick that bombed?"

"Oh, that." Kyle's eyes widened. "She still remembers that?"

"The Jinx never forgets anything," Adam assured him.

"I looked and looked for it," Jessie said, walking over. "But I couldn't find it. Are you sure it's in the field?"

"Uh . . ." said Kyle. "Uh . . . well . . . uh
. . . maybe it magicked itself *up* somewhere, like
. . . uh . . . in a tree!" he finished brightly.

Adam groaned. He could have thought of
something better than that. "Dumb," he whispered behind his hand.

Jessie didn't think it was dumb. "In a tree?"
she asked. "The magic duck egg's in a tree? How
can it get up in a tree? Does it fly?"

"It doesn't have to fly," Adam cut in. No
sense letting Kyle have all the fun. "It can probably just appear like magic in the air."

"Right," Kyle nodded. "In its magic nest."

"Hey, cut the talking!" Mark yelled. "Let's
get going. Take one!" He held up his camera.

"What do I do?" asked Jessie.

"You're supposed to faint," Mark called.
"When I count to three, you fall down, okay?"

"We're gonna do the attack scene." Adam
grinned his wickedest grin. He spat into the
weeds, then started toward Jessie, spreading his
cape out behind him.

"Ooooligaaan," he moaned, waving his arms
up and down.

Jessie's eyes went big and white. A thrill of
triumph shot through Adam. Guess he knew how
to ooligan someone. He made great swooping

41

dives, beating a zigzag path toward Jessie.

"One . . ." called Mark, zooming closer, "two . . . three. *Fall!*"

Jessie crumpled to the ground, throwing out her arms. "Ugh—got me," she groaned. "Did I do it right? Did I faint good?"

Mark whirred the camera on her. "Great! Now make the getaway, Adam."

Adam raced away, his cape billowing behind him. Mark ran after him, camera whirring.

"I'm done fainting!" Jessie shouted. "Now what do I do?"

"That's all. You're finished," Mark called back.

"*What!*" Jessie scrambled up. "I'm not done!" she screamed. "That wasn't anything!"

"Your job was to faint. You fainted. You're done."

"I'm supposed to be a princess!" Jessie hollered. "Princesses don't just lay there." She stamped her foot. "It's a *dumb* movie!" She ran over to grab Waffle Ann. "A stupid movie!" She spat into the bushes, a great big mad spit. "Miss Lynn knows more about princesses than you do! They *do* things! They find golden duck eggs!"

She turned toward the field. "Come on, Waffle Ann," she said in her loudest, maddest voice. "We can be princesses without them. We can find the golden duck egg."

She started toward the field, then stopped. There was a tall person in an orange vest moving over by the driveway.

Headhunters on one side—ooligans on the other. It was a dangerous world. Jessie turned and ran toward home.

# 7
# The Threat to Den 4

"It's going to be the best movie ever," Adam bragged at breakfast. "We've got great scary scenes. I really zapped Jessie, and Mark got it all on camera!" He poured himself a second bowl of cereal. "I bet the den picks my movie to show at the Blue and Gold Banquet!"

"I'm glad you let your sister be in the movie," Mom said. "That was generous, Adam."

Adam smiled virtuously through his Cheerios.

"He wathn't either nithe!" Jessie cried, sliding into the kitchen like always, on the holey feet of her pj's. "He wathn't nithe at all! He wath thupid!"

Adam looked up curiously. Did she forget how to talk overnight?

Mom was staring, too. "Jessie, what's that in your mouth?"

"Brathes," lisped Jessie. She smiled, showing a crooked wire thing hanging between her lips and teeth, flapping around when she talked. "I've got brathes, like Mark."

"It's a paper clip!" Adam whooped. "Jessie paper clipped her teeth!"

"Jessica Simpson, you get that paper clip out of your mouth this instant—before you cut your lips and scratch the enamel on your teeth!" Mom cried.

"I *need* brathes." Jessie backed away, covering her mouth. "My teeth are crooked."

"Your head's on crooked," Adam said.

"Jessie," Dad said in a slow patient voice, "braces are for older kids. And Cub Scouts are for older kids, too. There are lots of other fun things for five-year-olds. . . ."

"What?" Jessie demanded, staring at him. "What fun things?"

"Uh . . ." Dad said, "well . . . uh . . . there's the playground, and well . . . uh . . . when you're older, you can be in the Brownies." He looked over at Mom and grinned. "And your mom can be the leader!"

Mom didn't smile back. "It just so happens I talked to the scoutmaster yesterday. I told him he'd have to find another den leader."

Adam dropped his cereal spoon. "You mean . . . you *really* quit?" He never thought she'd do it. Not *really*.

"Not right away, Adam. I gave them till Christmas. Surely there's some other mom or dad who can take it then."

Adam got up and went to get his school books. He didn't want to sit and listen to Mom talk about quitting scouts. The den had to keep going. It was just getting good, now that the Jinx wasn't around for meetings, and now that his ooligan movie was going so well.

Dad didn't sound a bit worried. He acted like he thought the whole thing was funny. His voice boomed down the hall.

"Christmas, huh? And then it'll be just till Valentine's Day and then just till Easter. . . ."

"Christmas is my deadline," Mom cut in loudly. "If they can't find someone else, the den will just have to dissolve."

Adam gathered up his books. They'd find somebody. Sure they would.

"I'll let the kids have a sledding party in December," Mom went on, "Then, like I said, if no one else takes it, the den will have to dissolve."

The terrible conversation went on and on. But Adam didn't listen. He put on his jacket and blocked out the awful words. He was concentrating so hard on not listening that he almost bumped into the Jinx, who was standing stock-still in the hall. Staring. *The* stare.

"Adam, what doth ditholve mean?" she asked.

"Take out the stupid paper clip. I can't understand you."

Jessie obediently yanked out the wire. "What does 'dissolve' mean?" she said, staring at him, hard.

"Dissolve?" He frowned, trying to think of a way to explain it. "Well, like if you put sugar in lemonade or Koolaid, it melts. Yeah, that's it—melt."

Jessie's eyes got very big. "Dissolve . . . means . . . *melt*?" she whispered in a horrified voice.

"Yeah—so what's the big deal?"

She put her hand on his arm. "Poor Adam,"

she said in a quivery voice. "Poor Adam . . ." Then she stuck her paper clip back in and started down the hall.

Adam shook his head. "Two brain cells," he muttered to himself. "Maybe not even that many. Maybe only one."

# 8
## Pizza and Golden Eggs

Adam had to wait a whole month to show the ooligan movie to the rest of the den. First Mark got the flu, so they couldn't shoot the last scene. Then Mark's dad forgot to drop off the film to be developed. That wasted another week. Then it took time for the developing, and more time to synchronize sounds on tape to go with the film, so the movie wasn't ready until the den meeting on the day before Christmas break.

It was worth the wait. The clay figures didn't look much like prehistoric monsters, but everything else was terrific. Adam's fangs practically glowed; the black cape was pure Dracula. And the chase scene looked so good, Adam got shivers just watching it. Best of all, Jessie was blurred, so no one would be able to tell it was his little sister.

"Great show, Adam!" everyone cheered when the lights went back on.

"How did you make those monsters?"

"Not bad, Simpson!"

"I'm going to see if my dad'll let me use his video camera—that'd be even easier!"

No doubt about it. The best show in the den. They voted Adam's movie to be presented at the Blue and Gold Banquet in February.

"Now remember, boys," Mom said at least three times, as she closed the meeting, "we'll have a sledding party during the Christmas break— and that will be the last meeting, unless one of your parents can be a den leader. So go home and work on them, all of you. Otherwise, there won't *be* a den."

"I already asked my mom," Trevor yelled out. "She said no way was she having a bunch of kids running all over the place every week." He grinned, like he'd said something clever.

"My mom works," said Steven.

"So does mine."

"My mom said she'd help, but she wouldn't be leader."

Adam bit his lip and stared at the movie projector, still set up along the wall. Mom couldn't quit now! If the den broke up, he wouldn't get to show his movie, or go to Scout camp this summer, or be in the Scoutarama. And every year, the whole pack took a trip to Six Flags. . . .

Kyle wasn't worrying about the den at all. "No school for two whole weeks!" he whooped, as he walked with Adam to pick up Jessie at Miss Lynn's. "*And* no homework. *And* I get to stay overnight at your place."

"*And* we're having pizza," Adam jumped over the little plastic Santa by the Abernathys' trailer. "*And*—your mom can be den leader." He whirled to face Kyle. "You've got a bigger trailer than we do; it has a family room. And your mom doesn't work. It'd be perfect!" Why hadn't he thought of it before?

"She's having a baby in March," Kyle said. "Remember?"

"So what?" Adam said. "A baby'd be *easy*. It'd just lay there and sleep." A baby couldn't wreck a magic show or butt into a movie or anything. "It'd be better to have a baby around than my sister."

No one answered the door at Miss Lynn's when Adam banged on the teddy bear knocker. "Nobody home," he said cheerfully. "Maybe Miss Lynn kidnapped her and took her to South America."

"Hey . . ." Kyle stared toward the field. "Do you hear something?"

Then Adam heard it too—faint voices coming from the other side of the little hill at the edge of the field.

"Let's go see," Kyle mouthed the words. They sneaked over to the hill, crouching low. The voices got louder.

"The terrible dragon turned toward the princess. Fire leapt from his nostrils. But the brave princess drew her sword and plunged it in the dragon's belly, again and again. . . ." It was Miss Lynn's voice. "Isn't this a great book, Jessie? I found it at the college bookstore. The princesses *do* things!"

"She was a brave princess!" Jessie's voice, high and squeaky.

Where *were* they? Slowly, carefully, Adam crept closer, lay flat in the weeds, and peeked over the hill.

Miss Lynn and Jessie were sitting on a car

seat behind the hill, mostly hidden in the dried weeds. No car, no wheels, no frame, nothing except the seat. And the two of them were snuggled together, reading a book, like they were in the middle of the living room or something. There were two teddy bears on the seat, too. They had on knitted sweaters and hats.

Was *this* where they spent their Wednesdays, during the Scout meeting? And was this where Jessie ran and hid when they were all chasing her after the magic show?

"Now there's a princess," Miss Lynn went on in a loud satisfied voice.

"I'm brave, too. I'm going to find the golden egg!" Jessie sounded like her teeth were chattering.

"That's a fine quest for a princess."

Kyle tugged Adam's shirt. "She *still* remembers?" he whispered incredulously.

"I told you. She never forgets anything. She's part elephant."

"Maybe the magic golden egg will stop them from melting," Jessie said.

"Jessie, I think you heard wrong. Nothing's going to melt. Things are freezing. Like my poor fingers."

Kyle tugged Adam's sleeve. "You know," he whispered, "if she's gonna keep looking for the stupid egg, we could put one somewhere, for her to find. We could fool her."

"Oh sure," Adam whispered back, "and where are we gonna find a golden egg?"

"Well, maybe we could squish some aluminum foil—"

"That's silver. And it wouldn't look like an *egg*, dummy."

"Or . . . or . . . hey, I know!" Kyle yanked Adam farther down in the weeds. "My mom's been saving those eggs they put panty hose in— the silver and gold kind. She makes Christmas ornaments with them. We could put a gold one somewhere, and leave clues, like a treasure hunt. Really fool her!"

"Jessie can't read," Adam said automatically. But it did sound kind of fun. It'd be a real good joke. . . .

"Somebody could read it to her," Kyle said. "Or we could draw a picture or something. I'll go get the egg from my trailer and my sleeping bag too."

"Come right back," Adam hissed, as they started sneaking back away from the hill. "We can work on the hunt right after dinner."

"Pizza and golden eggs," Kyle giggled and ducked through the weeds toward home.

"Adam, where's Jessie? I told you to go bring Jessie home! Dinner's ready."

"She wasn't in the trailer, Mom. She and Miss Lynn were out in the field and . . ."

The door opened and Jessie walked in, stiffly, like a frozen robot. She didn't even take off her jacket or hat, just climbed up into her chair for dinner, looked at everyone, and said in a low whisper, "The headhunter collects heads."

There was a moment of silence while everyone thought about that. Dad was the first to speak.

"Makes sense," he said matter-of-factly. He picked up a piece of pizza. "A headhunter would."

Kyle giggled. Adam rolled his eyes. It'd be nice to invite a friend over to a nice *normal* kind of dinner conversation.

Mom turned to Jessie. "Honey, what in the world are you talking about? And you need to get out of your jacket."

Jessie kept sitting there. "The headhunter collects heads," she said again in a hushed, respectful voice. "Miss Lynn and me just saw him and he told us he collects heads."

Kyle giggled again. Mom and Dad still looked blank.

"It's Mr. Saunders," Adam explained, with a long sigh. "She calls him the headhunter. Because of the deer head. Remember?"

"There're other heads, too," Jessie whispered. "He told us. He has a bear head and a fish head and a bird . . . and . . . and heads all over!"

Kyle hiccupped. He stuffed in a piece of pizza and leaned over, staring hard at the table. His shoulders shook. Poor Kyle. It was awful to get the giggles at someone else's house. Just watching him made Adam start to giggle, too.

"I'm going to dream about those heads," Jessie announced, pulling off her hat. Like she planned her dreams every night. "Miss Lynn says princesses aren't scared of awful things. She got a new fairy tale book and it had brave princesses. They kill dragons." She shook her head sadly. "I don't kill dragons. I dream about heads."

This time Kyle's hiccup shot out a piece of pepperoni. Adam glanced sideways at him. Kyle looked like Mount Saint Helens, about ready to explode. Adam clamped his hand over his mouth and bent over his plate.

"Adam . . ." Mom shot him a warning look. Then she turned to Jessie. "Now, Jessie, if you think about other things—*nice* things—then you'll probably dream about them. Think about Christmas," she went on cheerfully. "We've got cookies to make and presents to wrap." She looked at Adam and Kyle. "Speaking of presents, don't forget to find a toy for the poor children, to bring to the collection box at the school hall."

Adam didn't trust himself to talk. He nodded helplessly.

"Who are the poor children?" Jessie asked.

"They're the boys and girls whose parents don't have much money, so they can't afford to buy them toys," Mom explained.

Jessie set down her pizza. "They don't have any toys?" she whispered in horror. She stared at Mom. *The* stare.

"Some don't. So it's nice if we share toys with them," Mom said. Then she looked out the window in surprise. "It's starting to snow! Maybe we'll have a white Christmas after all!"

"You can think about snow." Dad winked at Jessie. "Think about sledding in the morning." He and Mom went over to the front window.

Adam leaned close to Jessie. It was dangerous to try to talk. His voice wobbled. "You can th-think about snow and heads," he whispered, low so Mom couldn't hear. The wicked ooligan feeling was coming on. "Heads in the snow. Big fat heads rolling in the snow. . . ."

"A head on a sled," choked Kyle, stuffing his napkin in his mouth and rocking back and forth.

"A big red head on a sled," Adam gasped. Tears ran down his face.

"A big fat red head that's *dead* on a sled."

"A big fat red head that's dead because it *bled* on the sled. . . ."

"*Adam Simpson! Stop teasing your sister this instant!*"

The boys ran red-faced and giggling from the kitchen.

# 9
## Cookies and Clues

Kyle pulled the gold panty hose egg out of his pack.

"Here," he hiccupped, waving it at Adam. "Did you ever see anything else that looks more like a golden egg?"

"We need a clue. It's got to be easy. She only has two brain cells."

"I know!" Kyle recited:

> "The egg is not on a bridge.
> Go look in the fridge!"

Adam groaned. "Give it up, Anderson."

Kyle just hiccupped again. "Here's another one:

> Roses are red
> Eggs are golden
> Your egg is in
> a place very colden."

"It's not going to be in the refrigerator!" Adam grabbed the pencil. "Here, I've got one:

> To find the golden egg,
> What place would be best?
> Maybe up high—like in a nest.

"How's *that*?" he bragged.

Kyle grinned. "A nest, huh? Are we really gonna put it in a nest?"

"The Christmas tree. With all those pine needles, it'll look like a nest, right? Anyway, that was the only way I could make it rhyme." He walked quietly to the doorway. "Now we have to find a place to put the clue." He felt very sneaky and Christmasy, walking down the hall with the clue hidden in his fist. Here he was practically creating a whole treasure hunt for the Jinx, giving her the thing she wanted most in the world. Pretty nice big brother, actually.

Mom's mood was not Christmasy.

"Drat these spritz cookies!" She banged down the cookie press. "Just look at these!" She glared from the cookies to Adam.

Adam peeked at the little blobs of dough. Usually they squeezed out of the cookie press in nice Christmas shapes, like trees or wreaths. But these looked like play dough.

"Uh . . . they'll taste good. . . ."

Mom stuck more dough in and pushed the plunger down. More dough squeezed out, but instead of dropping on the cookie sheet in nice shapes, it stuck to the plunger.

"Would you cooperate!" Mom yelled at the cookie press, like it was Jessie or Adam. "I don't have time for problems. I've got too many cookies to make!"

Adam started backing out of the kitchen, and ran into something with two legs on the bottom and four big rolls of wrapping paper on the top. Jessie fell on the floor and the wrapping paper rolled all over the place.

"Hey, watch where you're going!" he yelled.

"I couldn't see where I was going."

"That *does* it!" Mom's yell was louder than both of theirs. "No spritz cookies this year, kids."

Jessie scrambled up and ran into the kitchen.

"We always have spritz cookies!" she cried. "I want them!"

"They're not working. Nothing works when you're in a hurry." Mom wiped the cookie press with a towel and set it down on the counter with a thud. "There. I don't even want to *look* at that thing again." She marched out of the kitchen.

Mom didn't usually get that mad at cookies. Adam looked at Jessie. The Jinx was staring hard at the cookie press.

"Hey, what's going on?" Kyle hissed down the hall.

Adam looked at Jessie again. She was still staring at the cookie press. Something was going on with those two brain cells. But he didn't have time to worry about it now. He hurried to his room.

"Jessie's still in the kitchen," he whispered. "Quick—we can put the note in her room. On her doll. She'll find it there for sure."

Waffle-face was sitting on the bed, chin deep in Christmas paper. There were about a zillion pieces of ribbon all over the place. Kyle started to attach the note. "Hey, what's that on her mouth?"

Adam looked closer and groaned. "Paper clips!" Waffle Ann got braces too. Oh well, poor doll was used to torture.

Adam pinned the note on the orange scarf around Waffle Ann's neck. "There. Now let's put the golden egg in the Christmas tree before she gets back."

The way they were sneaking around and whispering, it really felt like a big Christmas secret. Adam wasn't even sure anymore if the whole thing was a joke . . . or a present.

They set the panty hose egg on a thick wad of pine needles on one of the middle branches of the tree and headed back to Adam's room. Adam stopped in the doorway.

Jessie was there, bending over his rug. She stood up quickly, with her hand behind her back.

"What're you doing in my room?" Adam yelled. He took a step toward her. "What did you get? Let me see!"

"Nothing, nothing, nothing!" Jessie yelled, slipping out around him. "I didn't take *nothing*! I was just only looking for something!" She dashed out the door.

"You better be just looking!" Adam yelled after her. "Stay out of my room!"

"Go in your own room," Kyle added. "Look for things in *your* room. Maybe you'll find something there."

But the hint didn't help. Her room was so

full of wrapping paper and ribbons and tape, that she didn't even *find* the note that night. They waited and waited, all the way through the late show—and then she woke them up, running down the hall the next morning.

"Waffle Ann got a letter! Waffle Ann got a letter!"

"Really?" Kyle said in a very surprised voice, rubbing his eyes and propping himself up in his sleeping bag.

"I'll read it for you," Adam volunteered, yawning.

"In a tree! My golden egg's in a nest in a tree!" Jessie jumped up and down with excitement. "What tree?"

"Maybe the Christmas tree," Adam hinted. They followed her as she went tearing down the hall and over to the tree, pushing and shoving at the branches, knocking off ornaments, searching.

Adam couldn't believe it. It was so *obvious*, all golden and egg-looking, sitting right in front of her nose on the front branch!

"Look, Jessie, there it is!" He finally got tired of waiting. "A golden egg!"

"*Wow!*" cried Kyle.

"That? That's just a panty hose egg," Jessie

grabbed it and pulled it apart. "See?" she said as a bunched-up wad of brown fell on the rug. She picked it up. "See?" she said again. "Mommy puts hose in it. It's not magic."

Adam groaned. "You forgot to take out the *hose*," he hissed behind his hand to Kyle. Then he turned to Jessie.

"That's it! It's golden; it's an egg; it's in a tree, just like the note says. What more do you want? It's a great egg!"

"Then you can keep it." Jessie handed it to him and ran out of the room, leaving Adam standing there with the two pieces of egg and the panty hose. She was back two seconds later, with her jacket over her pajamas, and a package under each arm.

" 'Scuse me. I'm delivering presents," she said, heading for the door. Then she turned. "Adam, know what I want for Christmas? I want a spit wad refrigerator. Just like yours."

"Well, you're not getting it! You're not getting anything!" Adam threw the egg on the floor. He felt cheated, grouchy, still half-groggy. All that work. All that *work* to get her the golden egg, and what did she want? His spit wad refrigerator!

"Well," Kyle said, staring forlornly at the

pieces of egg on the floor, "we tried."

Adam kicked the egg under the tree. That was the Jinx for you. She could jinx a Scout meeting, she could jinx a magic show, she could even jinx her own surprise.

# 10
# The Extra Present

After dinner that night there was a knock at the door. Miss Lynn stood there with a big plate full of cookies.

"Merry Christmas!" she said and held out the plate.

Adam threw the door open. "Come in! Hey, Mom, *her* spritz cookies turned out great!" Some were in Christmas tree shapes, some were wreaths, some were made of chocolate dough, and some were covered in red and green sprinkles. Adam grabbed a chocolate one.

"I'd been wondering what kind of cookie to make for Christmas this year," Miss Lynn said. "So when Jessie left the cookie press package, it was just too tempting. Thanks for loaning it, Jessie. And for wrapping it so nicely. I brought it back safe and sound." She set the box on the table.

Adam stopped chewing. He looked at Jessie in disbelief. The Jinx gave away Mom's cookie press! Wrapped it up and gave it to the neighbor! No wonder Jessie was all scrunched down in her chair, looking guilty.

"You said you didn't want to see it anymore," she whispered.

Mom was playing it cool, saying, "Thank you—sit down—how are things at the college," as if people wrapped up her cooking stuff and gave them away for presents all the time.

Dad wasn't saying anything, just staring at Jessie with one eyebrow raised.

"Yoo-hoo, anybody home?" a deep voice called out from the back yard. Adam ran to open the door.

Mr. Saunders stood there in his orange hunter's vest. He was holding a big fat candy cane wrapped in cellophane.

"The headhunter!" Jessie whispered and scrunched down even lower.

"Shh. . . . His name is Mr. Saunders," Mom said in a low voice.

"Come in!" Adam called. This was turning into a regular party!

"I just came over to thank Jessie for the present," Mr. Saunders said. "I probably wouldn't have figured out who it was from, if I hadn't seen Lynn this afternoon. She got a present, too." He grinned and held up a doll's head.

Adam felt his mouth open so wide the cookie almost fell out. "A doll's head!" he yelped. "She gave you a *doll's* head? What a *dumb* present!"

"Not a dumb present at all," Mr. Saunders said, giving Adam a little wink. "And I brought a present over, too." He held out the candy cane. "You two can share it."

"The present's for your head collection," Jessie was still whispering. "She used to be Miranda."

Adam groaned. "I'm making a new Christmas list. I'm asking for a sister with more than two brain cells."

Mom's face was a little red. But she was still playing it cool. "Uh . . . would you like a cookie, Bruce?" her voice almost sounded normal. Dad stared at the doll's head, then at Jessie, and shook his head.

"No, thanks," Mr. Saunders said. "I've got to get back. My church group is caroling at the hospital. We drop off donated toys every year."

Jessie jumped up. "You mean toys for the poor children? You know where the poor children live?" she cried eagerly. She turned and ran to her bedroom and came zooming back, waving a package.

"Here. This is for a boy," she said, handing it to Mr. Saunders. "It's a car."

"A car!" Adam cried, staring at the package. "Where'd you get that?" Even as he said it, he knew where she'd got it. And why she had been in his room last night.

"Don't be selfish, Adam," Jessie said sternly. "You have lots of toys. And the poor children don't have any!"

"At the rate you're going, I'll be just like them," he muttered. Then, in a louder voice, "Go ahead. I don't need it." What else could he say? He aimed another glare at her. Weird sister—now she was scratching like a monkey.

"Mighty generous of you." Mr. Saunders gave Adam another wink. Then he turned to Mom. "Say, the little girl was telling Lynn and me that you're going to have a sledding party.

You're welcome to use the big hill behind my place."

Adam felt his spritz cookie tumble to the pit of his stomach. Suicide Hill. He was letting them use Suicide Hill. And Mom was saying, "Thank you, the kids'll have a great time. . . ."

He would not have a great time. He wanted to sled down Suicide Hill about as much as he wanted to broadjump the Grand Canyon. The hill didn't get its name for nothing.

"Now wasn't that nice of Bruce to let us use his hill for the party," Mom said after he and Miss Lynn left. She picked up a cookie and nibbled at it, staring at Jessie.

"My but you've been a busy girl today, Jessie," she said. Adam couldn't tell from her tone if she was ready to laugh or get mad at Jessie. "And what else have you given away, besides your brother's toys and my cooking set?"

Dad shook his head. "The cookie press, a toy, and a *doll's* head."

"Nothing else," Jessie said in a tired, whiny voice. "We're all out of wrapping paper." She plopped down backward onto the couch and started scratching again. "I don't feel good."

"What's the matter? Got fleas?" Adam asked.

Mom checked Jessie's stomach. "Oh dear." She picked her up. "We better get you to bed, little elf. Looks like someone gave you an extra Christmas present. The chicken pox."

# 11
# December: The Cub Scout Sledding Party

"Quit cheating!" Adam cried. "You're only supposed to move the red ones. I told you that three times!" He turned to Mom. "Why do I have to play checkers with her? I need to get ready for the sledding party."

"It won't hurt you to be a little nice to your sister, Adam Simpson," Mom said sternly. "Remember, *you* get a party today, and Jessie has to stay home with the chicken pox."

Adam groaned. "She doesn't even know the rules!" He moved his black checker and double-jumped Jessie.

"Quit taking my checkers!" Jessie grabbed them back. Then she moved her red checker in a giant kangaroo leap halfway across the board and scooped up four of Adam's checkers. "I jumped you!" she sang out.

"Quit cheating! You can't do that. I told you how to move!" He gave her his fiercest glare.

The doorbell rang. "I'll get it!" Adam grabbed his coat on the way.

Kyle and Michael stood at the door.

"Do we really get to use Suicide Hill?" Michael asked right away.

"Yep," Kyle answered for Adam. "Mr. Saunders said so. He said he's going to start letting kids use it, now that he's retired and he's around most of the time."

"That's great! It's the best hill around!"

"Come on!"

"We can't sled till Steven's mom gets here," Adam muttered. "She's in charge." He didn't even want to think about Suicide Hill, much less go down it.

"I want to go, too!" Jessie stood by the door, holding her zipper bag of checkers. "I don't want to stay here and do games!"

"Yipes! Chicken pox!" Kyle yelped, holding

his sled in front of his face like a shield. "Get away or we'll catch it!" He and Michael both took off running through the snow, toward the field.

"I want to come too! My chicken pox is almost gone!"

"Bye, Jessie." Adam grinned wickedly. "Too bad you can't come sledding. Have a good time watching TV." He started after Michael and Kyle. They had stopped at the edge of the field and were staring up at Suicide Hill.

Adam stared too. It was high, white, sparkly—and steep. His stomach did a little flip.

"Hey, look, Trevor's already sledding!" Michael cried. "Let's go!"

"We're supposed to wait till Steven's mom gets here," Adam repeated, stubbornly. "Let's build a snowman or something, while we're waiting." He started rolling snow into a ball.

Kyle leaned over to pack a ball of snow, then he dropped it and picked up his sled again. "There's Steven's mom now!" he cried. "Come on, Adam. You can build a snowman anytime."

"Yeah," Adam said, but he kept on rolling snow. He finished the big ball for the bottom part, then the middle ball. He spent a long time on it, packing the snow carefully and smoothing it out.

"How come you don't want to go down the hill, Adam?" Trevor called out.

"None of your business!" Adam yelled back.

"Try it, Adam," Kyle said. "Suicide Hill's great."

Adam looked up at the hill. His stomach tightened into a fist. "Later," he said and threw a snowball at Kyle.

"What are you, scared or something?" Trevor said loudly.

"Shut up, Trevor," Kyle yelled.

Trevor ignored him. "Are you scared to go down the hill, Adam?" he said again, smiling a mean smile.

Adam spat into the snow. He yanked his mittens off and took a step toward Trevor. "I'll sled when I want to." He could make his voice mean and tough, too. "Wanna make something of it?"

Trevor looked down. "Chicken," he muttered, taking a half-step back.

Adam lunged forward. "Who you calling chicken!"

Trevor turned to run. Adam grabbed his jacket by the pocket. There was a tearing sound. Trevor tripped and went down, with Adam tumbling on top.

"Fight! Fight!" Suddenly the whole den was standing in a circle in the snow, yelling and jumping.

"Get him, Adam. C'mon, give it to him!"

"What's going on here? Stop that fighting this instant!" Steven's mom came running up. Then another voice broke in, calling from the field.

"Jessie! Jessie, where are you?"

Adam got up, brushing snow from his face, just as his mom came in sight.

"Have any of you seen Jessie?" she cried, panting. "She's not in the trailer! I can't find her anywhere!"

"She's not here," Adam muttered, still glaring at Trevor.

"Yes I am," said a small voice. Everyone stared as Jessie suddenly crawled out from under a pine tree.

"I'm here," she whispered again and stuck her finger in her mouth.

"Jessica Simpson!" Mom exploded. "What are you doing out here in the cold and snow with the chicken pox!"

"Nothing," Jessie whispered.

Adam opened his mouth to yell "Go home;

this is our party." He still felt mad, and his arm was sore, where he fell on it. But then he shut his mouth. Jessie didn't look so good. She looked almost asleep on her feet. Her eyes were funny. Under her ski cap, her face was all spotted.

But Kyle and Michael and the rest were all dancing around yelling "Help! Chicken pox! Get her out of here!"

"Settle down, boys!" Mom sounded tired and mad. "I told you, Jessie's not contagious anymore."

"Yes I am," Jessie's voice was a hoarse stubborn whisper. "My chicken pox is too catchy. Mr. Snow Pox caught it." She pointed.

There, behind a small pine tree, was the snowman Adam had made. Only he wasn't just two balls of white snow anymore. There were red things all over him.

"Wha—" Adam walked closer. "Checkers?" he cried in amazement. Then in a louder voice, "Jessie put checkers all over the snowman!"

"He's got the chicken pox," Jessie walked toward him, then plopped down in the snow and rubbed her eyes. "He's got it real bad. He can't come to the party till he gets better."

Adam kept staring at the snowman.

"Checker pox," he giggled. "The snowman's got the checker pox!"

"He better not scratch." Now Kyle was giggling, too. "Or they'll all fall off!"

"Checker scabs!"

"It's *chicken* pox!" Jessie started crying. "It's *catchy!* He's Mr. Snow Pox!"

"Shh, Jessie, it's all right." Mom picked up Jessie like she was a baby. "I think we better get you back to bed. Oomph, you're heavy in all these clothes!"

Suddenly Adam had a fantastic, terrific, wonderful idea. "Hey, Mom, do you want to pull her back in my sled?" he said eagerly. "Then you won't have to carry her!"

Mom looked surprised. "Thanks, Adam. That's very thoughtful of you. But this is your sledding party. You'll need it."

"No I won't," he said in his most generous voice. "I'm done sledding." He scooped up a handful of snow, eyeing Trevor.

"You can go ahead and take Jessie home," Steven's mom said. "I'll keep things going here." She looked at Trevor and Adam. "I'm sure we'll all get along just fine. Won't we, boys?" There was a warning note in her voice.

"Yeah, sure." Adam hid his snowball behind his back. There were lots better things to do in the snow than sledding.

"Bye," he cried cheerfully, watching Mom pull Jessie back in his sled. No sled, no Suicide Hill. He threw his snowball in the air.

Saved by the Jinx and her chicken pox!

# 12
# January: Melting Time

"Hey, Mom, guess what? Kyle's mom said she'd take the den, at least for awhile!" Adam burst into the room, breathlessly. "Me and Kyle finally talked her into it! She's coming over right now to talk to you about it." He held open the door. "Come on in! My mom's home," he hollered.

Mrs. Anderson was getting really big. She kind of waddled when she walked. Kyle ran in ahead of her.

"Hey, calm down, you two," Kyle's mom laughed. "I only said I'd get you ready for the

Blue and Gold Banquet. That's all. Someone else will have to take over after that."

"But that's wonderful!" Mom said, beaming. "You've no idea how much I appreciate this."

"With the baby coming in March, I really can't do it the whole year," Kyle's mom said.

"Well, the banquet is one of the high points of the year," Mom said. "If the den has to dissolve after that, it won't be quite so bad."

At the word "dissolve," Jessie looked up from her coloring book.

"Adam—" Jessie began.

Adam looked at her. Jessie had set down her crayons and was staring at him. *The* stare. The two-brain-cells-doing-a-double-Ferris-wheel-turn stare. When she spoke, her voice was quivery. "How do you stop things from melting?"

"What?" Kyle said.

"How do you stop things from melting?" Jessie said in a louder, even more trembly voice.

Kyle giggled. "You put them in the freezer."

Jessie stared at both of them so hard that Adam looked down to see if he'd gotten ketchup or something on his shirt.

"They . . . won't fit," Jessie said finally. Then she turned toward the window and pointed. "Like Mr. Snow Pox. He's melting."

"Oh, *that*," Adam said. "Snowmen always do that, dummy. It's no big thing."

"It always happens after Christmas," Kyle said wisely. "Things are supposed to melt then."

"No!" Jessie cried. "They're not supposed to!"

Adam blinked. He and Kyle looked at each other. Adam shrugged. There was no figuring the Jinx's mind.

"Look," he said with a sigh, "it's going to get colder again, and you'll wish it didn't. Just wait."

Jessie turned on the stare again. Full power. "You mean, if it gets colder, things won't melt?" she asked, very slowly.

"You got it," Kyle said cheerfully. "When it's cold, they freeze. When it's warm, they melt. Get it?"

"Uh-huh. I get it," Jessie said with a big smile.

"Who put the ice cubes in my milk?" cried Adam at dinner. He picked up his glass and shook it. Ice cubes clanked and milk drops splattered. "Look! It's all watery!" He pointed at Jessie. "You did it, didn't you?"

"Jessie," Mom said in a warning voice, "did you . . ."

"I just wanted to make his milk cold," Jessie whispered.

"Speaking of cold," Dad said, "is anyone besides me freezing in here? What's the thermostat at, anyway?" He got up and went into the living room.

"Good Lord! We're down to fifty-nine degrees in here! Jessie, have you been fooling with the dial again?"

"I was making it cold," Jessie said in a small voice.

"What do you think we are—penguins or something?" Adam cried. "I'm going to get my sweatshirt." He stomped down the hall and stopped short at the door to his room.

His bedspread was gone. And all his blankets. His sheet was a crumpled mess, and all the stuff that used to be on his bed was scattered all over the floor.

She might as well have left a sign that said, "The Jinx was here."

"Mom!" he hollered, running back to the kitchen. "Jessie took all the blankets off my bed!" He ran up to Jessie. "You trying to freeze me to death?" he demanded, grabbing her shoulders.

"No!" Jessie pulled back. "I just didn't want you to melt!" And she burst into tears.

Later, Adam had to lie on the sofa, his arms across his stomach. It hurt from laughing so hard.

Nobody, *nobody*, on the entire planet had a sister like the Jinx.

"Melt," he said weakly, his feet sort of kicking the air. "She was gonna freeze me. So I . . . wouldn't m . . ." he started giggling again. Ooh, his stomach hurt.

"Adam, control yourself," Dad was in the other chair, wiping his eyes. He'd finally stopped laughing.

"Now do you understand?" he said to Jessie in a sort of shaky voice. "Dissolve doesn't always mean melt. When Mom said the den was going to dissolve, she meant they wouldn't have any more meetings. That's all."

"Then how come Adam told me it meant melt?" Jessie demanded, sniffling. "He said it was like Koolaid."

"Well, he probably didn't understand your question."

"I didn't know she w-was talking about Scub . . . I mean Cub Scouts," Adam giggled. He stood up, holding his arms out straight, with the fingers pointed down.

"Drip, drip . . ." he moaned. "I'm not an ooligan now. I'm the drip monster. Drip, drip . . ."

he started sinking in a slow spiral, moaning and hissing. "Ooh, there goes my arm. Splash!"

"I think it was very considerate of Jessie to go to so much trouble for you, Adam," Mom cut in loudly. "Your sister cares about you. She was trying to protect you. She didn't want you to melt."

"I didn't want him to melt," Jessie agreed. "But if he *did* melt, I wanted his spit wad refrigerator."

"No!" Adam said through a hiccup. "First of all, I'm not going to melt. But if I did melt, my spit wad refrigerator would melt with me. And if it didn't melt with me, you still couldn't have it!"

"It's supposed to be for a dollhouse. It's not supposed to be for spit wads!" Jessie cried.

Dad shook his head. "Another five-year-old," he muttered. "We need another five-year-old in this trailer court. Then this kind of thing wouldn't always be happening."

"Anyway, Jessie," Mom said, "it's not for sure that the Cub Scouts will stop meeting. Remember, Kyle's mom said she'd take them for a while." She turned to Adam. "And someone else's mom might volunteer after that, who knows?" She lifted Jessie's chin. "Either way, you don't have to worry about it, OK?"

"OK," Jessie wiped her nose. "Can I go to the Blue and Gold Bank?"

"Banquet," said Dad.

"No," said Adam.

"Of course," said Mom, louder than both of them. "It's the nicest event of the whole Cub Scout year and—" she looked at Adam. "It's for the *whole family*."

# 13
## The Pom-Pom Girl

Adam was shoveling snow when he saw the new trailer. It was a supercold day. All the snow that had melted during the thaw had refrozen into slippery hard lumps, making the whole trailer court like a bumpy ice skating rink. The new blue trailer was parked on the far side of the Aberna-thys'. There was a little kid playing outside.

She was wearing a yellow snowsuit, with a thick scarf bundled around her neck and a knitted hat with a big pom-pom. She was picking stuff off the sidewalk.

She looked about the same size as the Jinx.

The door to the trailer opened and a woman poked her head out. "Amber," she called, "don't play with the de-icer crystals. Leave them alone."

The door shut and then the little girl leaned over and started picking up the crystals again.

Adam grinned. This Amber was the right size; she didn't do what she was supposed to—she would be a perfect playmate for the Jinx! What had Dad said? If there was another five-year-old around, then Jessie wouldn't tag along after Adam. She'd find her own stuff to do.

He dropped his shovel and ran into the trailer.

"Jessie, hey Jessie, get your coat on. Come outside," he yelled.

"Why? What's outside, Adam?" Jessie scrambled up from in front of the TV.

"Here," he grabbed her coat off the hook and threw it at her. "There's a new trailer and there's a little girl your age outside playing."

"Really?" Jessie struggled into her coat, as she headed for the door. "A girl? My age?"

"Yep. Her name's Amber. Hey, watch out. It's all icy out here." He grabbed her coat sleeve as she skidded and wobbled and almost fell.

"Where?" Jessie demanded. "Where is the little girl named Amber?"

"There. See?"

Jessie looked. She looked so long that Adam's toes and fingers started to go numb from cold. He half-expected the little kid in the yellow snowsuit to vaporize under the stare. But she just kept right on picking up the de-icer crystals. And Jessie kept standing there, staring.

"She has a big yellow pom-pom," Jessie whispered at last.

Was *that* all she had to say?

"Go on." Adam gave her a little shove. "Don't just stand there like a jerk. Go say hi!"

Jessie put her mitten thumb in her mouth.

Amber looked up. She stared at Jessie. Jessie chewed harder on her mitten. Amber scuffed her boot back and forth. Jessie looked down, then peeked up again. Amber said something, looking down at her boot. Was it "hi"?

Adam groaned inside. Wouldn't you know, just wouldn't you know, the very one and only time she was supposed to talk and be friendly, she'd clam up? The same old Jessie who could single-handedly crash a whole den meeting, who dropped off doll heads on neighbor's porches and talked to grocery store clerks and mailmen and everybody else in sight. Here she stood, trying to swallow her mitten whole.

Well then, he'd take charge. He cleared his throat. "Jessie, that's, uh, Amber." He jerked his thumb at the yellow snowsuit. He raised his voice. "This is Jessie." He didn't know what else to say. Both girls were staring at him.

"Amber!" The door to the new trailer opened a crack. "Time to come in. It's too cold to stay outside." The door shut again.

Amber scuffed her boot harder. She mumbled something else. Was it "bye"? Then she turned and ran into the trailer.

Jessie stood there a second longer, watching the door, then she turned to Adam. "She had a yellow pom-pom!" she whispered eagerly. "A big yellow pom-pom!"

Dumb Jessie. Didn't even notice the *kid*—just her hat.

"Come on. Let's go back," he growled.

Jessie came to life then, slipping and sliding over the ice-lumpy sidewalk.

"A big yellow pom-pom," she repeated happily. She tugged at Adam's arm and just about pulled him over onto the ice.

"Thanks for meeting me to the pom-pom girl."

He threw up his hands in exasperation. There was no figuring the Jinx.

# 14
# February:
# The Blue and Gold Banquet

"So tonight we all get to see the great ooligan show," Dad said as he swung the car into the school parking lot.

"Yep." Adam climbed out. "Wait 'til you see the decorations we made!" He led them to the school cafeteria, bragging all the way. "Wait 'til you see the blue and gold placemats. And wait 'til you see the *piñata*! We get to break it after the potluck supper." He pulled open the door.

Blue and yellow crepe paper streamers trailed across the ceiling; blue and gold balloons hung in bunches over the tables, which were covered with blue and yellow tablecloths.

Mom set down her casserole on a long table at the front and turned to Adam with a little smile. "There's a surprise for you at the end of the program."

"What?" Adam asked instantly, but Mom just shook her head. "You'll see," she promised.

"Our den sits over here. We made place cards." Adam led them to a table that had a blue and gold peanut tree for a centerpiece. Blue and gold painted peanuts hung from a branch stuck in a coffee can. "After dinner every den is going to do something before we break the *piñata. That's* when we show the ooligan movie."

The microphone crackled. "Ladies and gentlemen, we're glad you could all come tonight. I think we can line up for the food now. . . ." The last words were drowned out by a stampede of blue and gold uniforms racing to the potluck table.

Adam shoved in with the rest of them. Such a feast! Tons of hot dishes, a whole tableful of salads, and the *desserts!* Cakes, brownies, cookies, more cakes, pies, more cookies, candy . . . Adam put only a few spoonfuls of spaghetti on his plate to save plenty of room for the desserts.

Jessie was already sitting eating her dinner

when he threaded his way back to their table. "Jessie, how did you get here so fast?" Mom cried. "I was looking all over for you. And what have you got on your plate?"

"She butted ahead of everyone," Adam mumbled through his spaghetti. "I saw her. She practically crawled under people's legs."

Mom was still staring at Jessie's plate. "Three cupcakes and four deviled eggs! That's no kind of dinner!"

"It's a great dinner," Jessie said, clutching her plate.

The microphone crackled again. "To speed things along, we're going to present some of the entertainment while you all enjoy your dinners," boomed the scoutmaster's voice. "Our first presentation will be a kazoo band from Den 7. If you kids can come up here—"

Adam smirked. Kazoos. Any kindergartner could play a kazoo. Just wait till they got to the ooligan show!

"My brother's a Scub Scout," Jessie waved her orange knee sock scarf at a little girl sitting across the aisle.

"*Cub* Scout," the little girl corrected her. "Not Scub Scout."

"See!" Adam jabbed Jessie with his elbow.

"See?" he hissed triumphantly. "Every other little kid can say it right. You're the only dumbo that says it wrong."

Jessie ignored him and turned to the little girl. "I know *that*," she said with great dignity. "Who doesn't know *that*?"

"Anyway, Cub Scouts are boring," the little girl said, tossing back her long curly hair. "They meet at our house and they do boring things."

Jessie's eyes got big. She stared at the little girl. *The* stare. Then she tossed back her own hair.

"Yeah," she said. "They sure are. Bo-ring."

The next two skits *were* boring. No one could even hear Den 2's puppet show. And Den 3's jug band was awful. "Just wait till my turn," Adam kept bragging.

"If we can have Adam Simpson up here," the scoutmaster called, "the last presentation will be a movie called 'The Ooligan Show.' We'll have to cut the lights; hope you can all find your food."

"That's me! I'm on!" Adam got up so fast his chair fell over. He ran to where the projector was set up at the back of the room.

"We now present 'The Ooligan Show!' " he cried.

"I'm in the movie," Jessie said to the little girl at the table. She tossed her hair back again. "I faint! Watch real good. You'll see me."

The lights went out. The projector started whirring. "Watch," Jessie whispered again. "Watch me faint."

The ooligan appeared on the screen, swooping and diving. He looked like Adam, with fangs.

Now there was something else on the screen. Something little. And yellow. Jessie leaned forward, squinting to see better. Was that *her*? She should look bigger, closer. Nobody would even know who that yellow person was!

Then the little yellow person fell down out of sight. And the Adam-ooligan filled up the screen again.

"It's a *dumb* show," Jessie whispered. "It doesn't even show me fainting. *Stupid* show!" She got up fast, almost knocking her chair over. "Princesses aren't supposed to faint, anyways. They're supposed to find golden duck eggs!" And she ran out of the room.

# 15
# The Rescue

The ooligan show was done. It was a great success. Much better than kazoo bands, jug bands, and puppet shows.

"Come on, let's be first in line for the *piñata*!" Kyle ran over to Adam and Steven. "If we leave now, we can get to the gym ahead of everybody."

"Everyone's supposed to help clean up—"

"So let's get out of here *fast* before they see us," Kyle hissed.

"Last one to the gym's a rotten egg!" Steven whispered.

Adam stopped partway down the hall. "Did you hear something?"

"Something fell!"

Then another sound came, faintly, from the gym. And a high-pitched yell that sounded like "help!"

"Somebody's hurt!"

"Hurry!" They half-ran, half-slid down the waxed hallway to the gym.

Adam stopped at the doorway. And stared.

"I don't believe it," he muttered. "I don't believe it. Yes. I do believe it."

"Help!" yelled Jessie. She was hanging from the *piñata* rope, her hands clutching a knot in the rope just below the basketball hoop, her feet kicking at the top of the *piñata*, spinning and twirling it. There was a ladder, half-fallen against the wall a few yards away.

"Help!" she squealed, kicking and twirling. "I'm falling!"

"Adam, it's your sister!"

"*Help!*" Jessie sobbed. "I'm *drowning!*"

Adam came to life. He ran over and shook his fist up at her. "Get down!" he cried. "You get down right now!"

"I *can't!* I'm too high!" she screamed. "I'm gonna fall! I'm gonna drown!"

"Stupid, you can't drown. There's no water!"

"I am too gonna drown!" Jessie yelled. Tears started rolling down her cheeks. "I'm gonna drown; I'm gonna fall! I'm gonna fall and drown!"

"You're going to break our *piñata*! That's what you're going to do!" Adam hollered back angrily.

"It's not a *piñata*! It's my golden duck egg! It's in its nest. I was trying to get it!"

Adam groaned. He whacked his hand to his forehead.

"That's how she got up." Kyle pointed to the ladder.

"And that's how she's gonna get back down, too!" Adam ran to the ladder. "Help me get this back up." Struggling, they managed to get it set up beside the rope, while Jessie kicked and twirled and hollered.

"Now climb down!" Adam called up to her. "Quit bawling and climb down!"

"I can't let go!" Jessie screamed, kicking her legs. She sounded really terrified now. "Adam, get me down!"

"Stupid!" Adam growled. But she was right. Drat her, she really couldn't let go, or she'd fall. And it really would be a long drop to the gym floor. She'd probably break a leg or something. "Stupid," he muttered again, angrily. He hated ladders as much as he hated high tree limbs and high sled runs.

"My hands are slipping!" Jessie howled. "I'm *drowning*!"

She looked about ready to lose her grip.

"Hang on and shut up!" Adam yelled and stepped on the first rung. "Hold it steady," he hissed at Kyle and Steven. If they didn't hold tight, his shaking would topple it again.

Stupid Jessie. Stupid Jinx. Was there one thing, one single thing she didn't wreck?

He started climbing. His legs felt like they just got out of the blender. His nose itched. After he got her down, he'd kill her.

Second step from the top, he stopped. Now how the heck was he supposed to get her down, without falling himself?

"Keep the ladder steady," he called and reached out a hand to grab the rope.

"Help! You'll spill me!" Jessie yelled hysterically.

"Would you shut up!" Adam didn't like the shaky sound in his voice. What was he supposed to do now? There was more to this rescue stuff than he realized.

"Adam, grab her with one hand!"

"Jessie, reach for Adam! Grab him." Kyle and Steven yelled suggestions from the floor.

"I can't let go!" Jessie was whimpering now. "I'll *fall!*"

"You have to!"

Jessie made a sound like "YOOOOW!" and fell toward him, one hand pawing and clutching at him like a cat. The next second she let go of the rope with her other hand and crashed against him, arms and legs grabbing and pulling and pinching, like an insane octopus.

"Ouch! Let go. You're strangling me!" Adam yelped, then shut his mouth at a sudden burst of noise from the other side of the gym.

Clapping. Whistling. Yelling.

The Cub Scouts were down there. And other little kids.

"Adam got her down!" Kyle's voice.

"Ya-hoo!" Was that Steven? Teasing . . . but triumphant. And there were all those other kids, looking up at him, clapping—

Suddenly there was a great burst of people flooding the room.

"Who's stuck?"

"Where?"

"What's going on in here?"

Several men ran toward the ladder, crossing the gym floor in fast strides, reaching up, peeling the octopus off Adam, saying, "Easy now, stop crying, what happened, how did she get up there, you can climb down now, son."

Adam felt hands guiding him back down. He tried to jump to the floor from the second to the last step, but his legs weren't very reliable. He fell.

And Kyle and Steven and Michael were clapping him on the back and yelling, "Good job, Adam!" They were teasing, but meaning it at the same time.

"Jessie, your big brother rescued you!"

"Adam, things really happen when your little sister's around!" Kyle sounded amazed.

That could be the headline of the year: THE INCREDIBLE JINX STRIKES AGAIN. She should advertise: *Rent-a-Jinx. Guaranteed to wreck every occasion, rain or shine. No charge.*

Yep, Jessie had done it again. She'd jinxed the Blue and Gold Banquet, just like she'd jinxed everything else the whole year. He should feel really mad. He had every right to.

But . . . his eyes went to the rope and the knot, above the *piñata*. The ladder had been closed up and moved away. But in his mind he saw it standing there under the *piñata*, saw himself climbing up bravely toward Jessie, grabbing her. And all those people watching and clapping . . . A warm, proud feeling poured over him. He grinned.

"Adam, did you hear me?" Kyle waved his hand in front of Adam's face. "They're going to start the line to break the *piñata*!"

"Mmm . . ." murmured Adam, staring at the *piñata*, but again seeing the ladder; Jessie leaping toward him; people below clapping, clapping. . . .

# 16
# The Hatching
# of the Magic Egg

"They're hitting my golden duck egg! They're hitting it with a baseball bat! They're gonna kill it!"

"Jessie, listen, it's only a *piñata*. They're supposed to break it open."

"They're going to kill it!" She lay down on the gym floor and kicked her feet and pounded her fists and howled.

Wow. It was the first time Adam had ever seen the Jinx throw a real live tantrum. Usually she just fastened her laser stare on things and then got her way by figuring out something sly and sneaky. But this was something else. She was going to make herself sick. Nobody could keep up that kind of screaming very long.

Mom tried to shut her up. She got Jessie off the floor, but the Jinx was still swinging her arms and howling. More people were watching her than the *piñata*.

Dad tried to shut her up. Her howls got softer, but mostly because she was running out of air.

"It's *my* golden egg. I f-found it! Adam's clue said it was in a n-nest. There's the n-nest!" And she started howling again.

"Jessie . . . Jessie . . ." Mom and Dad both looked embarrassed.

Adam wished there was a hole in the floor he could drop through.

"You and your big ideas," he muttered to Kyle. "You started the whole stupid egg thing!"

"Oh yeah? Who wrote the clue about the nest?" Kyle shot back. Then he grinned. "You're the one who 'egged' her on."

"It's *my* golden egg! It's *mine*!!"

Adam was getting worried. If she kept it up much longer, she'd explode or crack up or something.

Why did she care so much about the dumb

egg? Why had they teased her about it?

Somebody had to stop her. He ran over to her, dodging her flailing arms and legs.

"Jessie, listen to me!" he yelled. "You're supposed to break magic eggs to . . . uh . . . to get the magic. Otherwise it . . . it, uh . . . can't come out," he said, thinking fast.

She broke off, mid-howl, and stared at him. Even through her red eyes and runny nose and hiccups, he recognized *the* stare. She was thinking. And two brains cells couldn't concentrate on a tantrum and this, too. Adam let out a sigh of relief.

"Wh-what?" she sniffled, staring at Adam.

"You're *supposed* to break the magic egg," he repeated. He felt a sudden burst of inspiration. "To hatch the magic. That's what they're doing with the baseball bat. Otherwise, the magic is . . . uh . . . stuck inside." He nodded, pleased with himself.

"The magic is . . . inside?" Jessie said slowly, still sniffling and gulping. "And . . . and you have to b-break it to get it out?"

"Right," Adam said.

Jessie hiccupped again, took a long deep gulpy breath, then another. She wiped her nose with her orange knee sock, then her eyes. Then, without another word, she marched across the floor and got in line behind Kyle.

It was Steven's turn. He made a small crack in the *piñata* when he gave it a mighty whack. There was a hopeful *cruuunch* sound. Lots of kids started forward. But no candy fell.

"Almost," Adam said. He punched Kyle. "Your turn. *Really* bang it. It's almost broke."

Kyle let the scoutmaster blindfold him, then he yelled "Geronimo!" and raised the baseball bat and gave a loud whack. But he was off center. The bat just hit the edge of the *piñata*. There was another small "cruuunch" sound. Still the piñata hung there, whole.

"Rats," said Kyle. "If I'd just been a little higher!"

"My turn," said Jessie. Her voice was still gulpy. "My turn, my turn."

She stood very still while the blindfold went on.

"I bet she can't even *reach* it," cried Trevor.

"Yes, I can too!" shouted Jessie and raised the baseball bat in a wild swing that pulled her off balance, so she almost fell over. She didn't even come close to the egg.

"Take off the blindfold. You missed the whole *piñata!*" yelled Trevor behind her. He started forward, then backed off quickly, as Jessie lifted the bat again.

"Hey!"

"Strike two!" she yelled and swung the bat again. She nicked the edge of the egg. The same place Kyle had hit.

"No fair!" several voices yelled. "She took two turns!" But Jessie ignored them and raised the bat again. "Strike three!" she cried and swung the bat so hard that she toppled onto the floor just as another *cruuunch* sounded above—

And candy poured down, raining all over the gym floor.

Kids surged forward, crawling, grabbing, yelling, running, shoving.

Jessie yanked off the blindfold. She stood very still, staring.

"My magic duck egg hatched candy," she whispered, slowly, as if in a daze. For another second she stood there, stock-still.

Then, with a little whoop, she dove down onto the floor.

# 17
## *The Surprise*

Candy, candy everywhere. Caramels, lemon drops, lollipops, gumdrops, wrapped toffees, peppermints . . .

Adam ran around madly stuffing candy everywhere—his mouth, his pockets, his socks, his fists. All the other kids were doing the same thing, except one, who was sitting right in the middle of the floor, holding the broken *piñata* shell, her hair sticking out in all directions, her face all smudged with tears, her orange knee sock undone and half-falling off her neck. Just sitting there, hugging the golden piece of *piñata*, with a big happy grin on her smudged-up face.

She was not like normal kids. But, like Kyle said, things *happened* when Jessie was around.

"If I can have your attention—" the scoutmaster called from the front of the room. "We cut short our announcements when we heard there was a problem here in the gym. But since some families are starting to leave, we have a few last announcements for you.

"First, we have some very good news to report. As some of you know, we've had trouble finding a permanent leader for Den 4. I'm pleased to tell you we now have a volunteer! He says he was recruited by a young lady in distress, young Jessie Simpson, who reported to him that her brother's den was going to . . . dissolve." The scoutmaster grinned.

Adam looked at Jessie. She was still hugging the piece of *piñata*, but she was looking up, wide-eyed, at the scoutmaster and at a second man walking up to the front. The man was tall and smiling and bearded, and he was wearing an orange hunter's vest.

"So folks," said the scoutmaster cheerfully, "before everyone leaves, let's have a big hand for the little girl who saved Den 4, and for its new leader, Bruce Saunders!"

Adam stared. Mr. Saunders was going to be den leader? Jessie's mouth fell open.

"The headhunter," she whispered.

Jessie sat in one corner of the back seat, hugging her golden egg. Adam sat in the other corner, chewing a caramel. He was looking out the window, but instead of the dark street, he was seeing again the gym, the rescue scene, the people clapping and cheering. He just loved to think about it. Each time it got better. Each time the warm proud glow spread over him like a blush, and he couldn't keep from smiling.

"I found my golden egg," Jessie whispered from her side of the seat.

"It's a *piñata*," Adam said automatically. "And you wrecked it. Jinxed the Blue and Gold Banquet, just like you jinxed everything else. Rode the *piñata*, hogged the baseball bat, threw a brat tantrum. . . ." But he couldn't summon up the proper mad feeling. The grin came back, hard as he tried to keep the corners of his mouth down.

"Adam, just remember," Mom said from the front seat. "It was Jessie who found the new den leader. I told you there'd be a surprise in store for you. And Jessie was the one who got Bruce interested. She saved the den."

III

"Let's hear it for the little girl who saved Den 4!" cried Jessie, clasping her hands around her egg.

"You didn't save anything. *I'm* the one who saved *you.*" Adam tried to sound very calm, matter-of-fact. He popped another caramel into his mouth and shot one toward her. It landed with a plunk right inside the broken *piñata* shell. "Hey, did you see that shot?" he bragged.

"Not bad," said Jessie.

They sat in the back seat like idiots, grinning at each other.

# 18
## "The Magic of the Egg"

"Now where are you going with that stupid egg?" Adam called, shoveling the new snow in the walkway. "You've already showed it to everyone in the whole trailer court."

"Not everyone," Jessie said, hugging her eggshell tightly, walking backwards to talk to him. "I only showed it to Miss Lynn and Mrs. Abernathy and now I'm going to show it to—"

"Watch out!" Adam called, but not fast enough. Jessie backed right into another little kid coming toward her. The new girl.

"Oops," Jessie said, trying to keep her balance. The two girls stared at each other.

Just like last time. Adam shook his head and bent over his shovel. Hopeless. Absolutely hopeless.

But then he heard a little girl's voice: "What's that?"

"It's my golden duck egg," Jessie whispered. "It's magic."

"Really?" The other little girl touched the egg. "Know what?" she said loudly. "There's a monster under our trailer. His name's Charles Patrick. You want to see him?"

"Really?" Jessie squeaked.

Adam shook his head. These two could qualify for the Guinness Book of World Records under "Dumbest Conversation." Now Jessie was spitting into the trash cans, a great big slobbery show-off spit. "I can spit as far as my brother," she bragged.

"So what? I can spit in different colors when I chew jellybeans."

Wow. Another person in this world just as wacko as the Jinx. Incredible. But—at least they were talking. Smiling. Running off together—

Adam crossed his fingers, as he headed back to the trailer. Maybe there *was* hope. . . .

\* \* \*

"Knock, knock. Anybody home?" Mr. Saunders's voice called into the living room. "Mrs. Anderson said you had some more Scout material for me."

Adam got up to let him in. Mom already had the box of materials ready. "Here it is," she said cheerfully. "I want to tell you again how much we all appreciate this."

"Well, now that I'm retired, I've got more time than I know what to do with." He set down the box and sank into the armchair. "I've been doing some thinking about what the boys would like." He looked at Adam. "I've got land up north. Thought maybe we could all go camping when the weather warms up."

"Really?" Adam half-jumped out of his chair. "That'd be *great!*"

"And I've got lots of little motors and gadgets in my shop. Maybe we could do some electronics projects."

Adam leaped up the rest of the way. "I love stuff like that! I've got batteries in my pocket—" He reached his hand in, emptying his pockets: a tiny screwdriver, two dimes, dirty Kleenex, a shrunken plastic head, his spit wad refrigerator, and down at the bottom, the two batteries. He'd planned to use them to make a battery-operated car sometime.

Jessie walked in from the kitchen. She was holding something in her hand. It was the same color as the knee sock she'd been wearing around her neck, but it was all cut up in a million strips, wadded together with a rubber band. She set the wad down on the table in the corner of the room, took out her ski cap, and started cutting a hole in the top.

Adam glanced over at Mom. But she was busy showing Mr. Saunders the Scout materials, not looking at the Jinx. Now Jessie was stuffing the wad of yellow strips into the hole at the top of her ski cap.

"My living room's plenty big for a bunch of boys to hold a meeting," Mr. Saunders went on. "And the kids might like the animal heads on the walls, from my hunting."

Jessie's head jerked up. "The room of the heads," she whispered. "Is Miranda's head up there, too? Is Miranda's head going to be a Cub Scout?"

Mr. Saunders winked at her. "Well, I don't know about your doll," he grinned, "but I think we ought to make a certain young lady here an honorary Cub Scout."

"Jessica Simpson!" Mom cried suddenly,